THE DUMP GANG

MARTIN WADDELL

Illustrations by

PAUL SAMPLE

WALKER BOOKS
AND SUBSIDIARIES
LONDON · BOSTON · SYDNEY

For the Bloomfields,
who lent me their mushrooms

First published 1995 by Walker Books Ltd
87 Vauxhall Walk, London SE11 5HJ

This edition published 2000

2 4 6 8 10 9 7 5 3 1

Text © 1995 Martin Waddell
Illustrations © 1995 Paul Sample

This book has been typeset in Plantin.

Printed in England by Clays Ltd, St Ives plc

British Library Cataloguing in Publication Data
A catalogue record for this book is
available from the British Library.

ISBN 0-7445-7245-2

Contents

The Bonzo Raid

The
Bonzo Raid

The Dump Gang First Team Squad was
Macmillan, Bo-Jeddy and Quinn. Macmillan
was three times bigger than anybody; Bo-
Jeddy was his sidekick, which isn't saying
much, and Quinn was *Quinn*, which says
quite a lot.

Everybody else around Worby Drive was in
one of the other gangs already, except Josie
Swab. Macmillan made a "No Girls" rule, so
Josie was out even if she'd wanted to be in,
which she didn't. Quinn reckoned Josie was
too smart to join any gang that had
Macmillan in it, but he didn't say so to
Macmillan. Bo-Jeddy pointed out that there
was room for only three in the Dump Gang
Hut anyway, so that settled it.

That was when the Dump Gang *had* a hut,
but one day they hadn't because the Bonzos

got onto the Dump and wrecked it.

It was Macmillan who found out what the Bonzos had done because he was first one along afterwards.

He came over the wire, under the trunk, down the pipe, round the back of the hedge and there was the hut ... wrecked. The Bonzos had kicked in the packing-case walls and pulled down the roof, and thrown Bo-Jeddy's spare-parts bike over the hedge into Eggy Marshall's allotment.

Old Eggy came out of his greenhouse, waving his stick.

"The Bonzos did it!" Eggy said.

"Right," said Macmillan.

"I nearly nicked them," Eggy said. "Only my legs don't go like they used to."

Macmillan gaped at him. Eggy was ultra-plus small, like a wizened peanut, and his little legs had gone bandy with age. The idea of Eggy chasing the Bonzos off the Dump took a lot of imagining.

Macmillan hopped over the wire, and got

the bike off Eggy's cabbages. He lugged it back over the wire, on to the Dump.

"Time something was done about them Bonzos," Eggy grumped.

"Yeah," said Macmillan, flexing his muscles, and he sped off to find Bo-Jeddy and Quinn.

They were in Monaco Amusements doing Crash Drivers.

Macmillan came diving in.

"Bonzos done our hut!" he shouted.

"Whaaaaaaa?" said Bo-Jeddy spinning round, and then remembering too late.

SMACK! The Dust Cloud got him. One minute he was PH 6/390.751 AV.SP./ O ELIM/83 S.P. and the next there were bits of his car all over the road and "YOU'RE DEAD MAN!" flashing blue and red all over the screen and the hooters going.

"Look at that!" said Bo-Jeddy in disgust.

Macmillan was too excited to be put off by the disaster.

"Bonzos done our hut," Macmillan yelled.

"We've got to get them, Bo-Jeddy!"

"Right," said Bo-Jeddy.

"Like *now*," said Macmillan.

Macmillan and Bo-Jeddy charged off to do it. They were charging out of the Monaco when they realized that Quinn wasn't with them, so they charged back again.

"Quinny!" they bawled at Quinn.

Quinn was still crouched over Crash Drivers.

"Shut up," he said. "I'm winning."

"Eh?" said Bo-Jeddy glancing up at the Rider Record on the screen. "PH 1 /093.005 AV. SP./2 ELIM./ O.S.P./RED WARNING and you're *winning*? That's not how it works."

"Oh, yes it is," said Quinn. "I'm still in the game, and you bombed out. So I'm winning, right?"

Bo-Jeddy reached out and hit the BIFF-JET PRO button. The next moment Quinn's Flash Speedster was in the Crocodile Swamp, and the machine was flashing "YOU'RE DEAD MAN!" with the hooters going and the crocodiles were eating Quinn.

Quinn went pale. It wasn't often he beat Bo-Jeddy on any machine, let alone Crash Drivers. Quinn's legs were too short to work the pedals properly.

"I'll get you for that, Bo-Jeddy," he said.

"Not now you won't," said Macmillan, pulling Quinn towards the door. "We got business with the Bonzos."

So Quinn didn't get Bo-Jeddy then. He saved it up for later.

They went to do the business on the Bonzos.

The Bonzos were down by the swings in John Bonzo Memorial Park, which was Bonzo Land. That is, Ratso and Meatface and Dummy and Marco were. Big Boots had to go home because of the dentist. Big Boots had wire teeth. He was always going to the dentist and the dentist never got it right but nobody felt sorry for Big Boots because Big Boots was horrible whether his teeth were straight or crooked.

"There they are," yelled Macmillan, and he broke into a sprint, running away from the others along the bike path towards the boating pond, and the swings. "Charge!"

"Death to the Bonzos!" yelled Bo-Jeddy and he was charging after Macmillan when Quinn grabbed him.

"Hold on, Bo-Jeddy," Quinn said. "Four Big Bonzos against us, right?"

"Yeah," said Bo-Jeddy.

"They'll kill us," Quinn pointed out.

"MACMILLAN!" they both yelled. But they were too late, because Macmillan had arrived in Bonzo Land.

It was really awesome watching Macmillan in action when he was mad.

Macmillan nearly did for the lot, all by himself. That is because Macmillan was so big, bigger than almost anybody in the world but Big Boots, and Big Boots wasn't there so he didn't count.

Macmillan just *went for it!*

So far as the Bonzos were concerned it was like being charged by a big, big, big gorilla. They took off through the bushes with Macmillan after them. Bo-Jeddy and Quinn were a long way behind. Then the Bonzos realized there was only Macmillan after them on his own.

He charged straight into a Bonzo ambush.

Ratso and Dummy grabbed one side, and Marco and Meatface got hold of him on the other, and they lifted Macmillan up and heaved him staggering towards the boating pond like four ants with a big twig.

They chucked Macmillan right into the drink.

There wasn't much water at that bit, mainly mud, so Macmillan didn't sink. He stumbled in up to his knees and then he sploshed about in the mud yelling, while the four Bonzos stood on the edge, calling him names like Mudpie and Dung Heap.

Quinn and Bo-Jeddy came creeping cautiously round the side of the bushes, and there were the four Bonzos standing right on the edge, stopping Macmillan getting out.

Quinn knew what to do the minute he saw them, and Quinn and Bo-Jeddy did the business.

It was e-a-s-y, e-a-s-y because they had two hands each between them, which is four hands, and the Bonzos were lined up close together. Quinn and Bo-Jeddy got up behind them and did a co-ordinated double shove, two-and-two makes four hands on four backs, one – two – three – four shove.

The four Bonzos landed face first in the mud and Macmillan sludged out of it.

Then the Dump Gang scarpered.

"Best Ever Numero Uno Victory over the Bonzos!" Bo-Jeddy boasted when they were well away.

"Yeah! Yeah! Yeah!" Little Quinny was bouncing around, punching the air. "Right in Bonzo Land too. Their territory!"

"Only I'm drippy up to the knees," said

Macmillan, looking down at his mud-covered jeans and wondering what his mother would say.

"It's worth it," gloated Quinn.

"Four Bonzos flat in the mud," cheered Bo-Jeddy. "Very worth it!"

"Yeah," said Macmillan, cheering up. "Ultra worth it!"

Even old Eggy Marshall agreed that it was when they told him, and Eggy wasn't easily pleased, but he reckoned the Bonzos deserved it for doing his cabbages with Bo-Jeddy's bike.

Macmillan went around boasting about Victory in Bonzo Land for days, although it wasn't really Macmillan that won it. It was Quinn's quick thinking that beat the Bonzos, not Macmillan's muscle.

"Macmillan's got a peanut brain," Bo-Jeddy said, disgustedly.

"Just don't tell him that if you want to keep your head," said Quinn. But he wasn't paying much attention. Quinn was busy figuring out how to get his own back on Bo-Jeddy for busting his Crash Drivers game. Quinn worked that way. Like an elephant, he never forgot.

Bo-Jeddy
in Pink Pants

Bo-Jeddy
in Pink Pants

One day Josie Swab was outside Quinn's
house waiting when Quinn came out.

"What do you want, Frogface?" Quinn
asked her, just to be friendly.

"I was waiting for you," Josie said,
advancing on him.

Quinn looked round, but there was
nowhere to run.

Josie wasn't just clever, she was tough as
well, and Quinn knew she'd got him cornered
as usual. It was a typical Josie Operation.

That was when Quinn made his big
mistake. He should have stayed in front of his
house, because as long as he was in sight of
the windows his mum might look out and
rescue him. He should have stayed, but he
didn't. He didn't want his mum to know he
needed rescuing from a girl, so he tried

getting away instead.

He started walking away, as quick as he could go without running, because he was in the Dump Gang and he wasn't going to be seen running from a girl, even if it was Josie.

He got round the corner out of sight, and *then* he started to run but he didn't get far.

Josie loped after little Quinn on her long legs and then she grabbed him and sat down on him.

"Eat gravel, Quinny!" Josie said, cheerfully pummelling him.

"You're breaking my back," Quinn yelled.

Josie bounced, and that stopped Quinn yelling.

"That's a good little boy," Josie said. "Dere, dere den."

"Get off!" Quinn panted.

Surprisingly, Josie got off, but she didn't let go. She yanked Quinn to his feet.

"Listen, Quinny," Josie said. "I want to do a deal with your gang."

Then she told him what the deal was.

"Oh no!" Quinn said.

"Oh yes," Josie said. "It's either you, Bo-Jeddy or Macmillan. One of you does it, or I'll see you all off."

Then she let Quinn go and tell the others.

"No way," said Bo-Jeddy, going pale.

"Not me neither," said Macmillan.

"She said either one of you would do," said Quinn. "She said I'm too small." The bit about Quinn being too small was a lie, of course, but the other two didn't spot it.

"She said if one of you didn't do it, she'd see us all off," Quinn went on.

"I'm too big," said Macmillan quickly. "It would look silly."

"Oh no, not me," said Bo-Jeddy. "Not me, no way. Me in pink pants?"

They ended up rolling Quinn to decide it. They rolled him off the top of the builder's sand and he finished up head first, so that decided it. Macmillan won, so Bo-Jeddy was it.

"I demand a re-roll," said Bo-Jeddy, but

Quinn wasn't going to get rolled twice. He had belted off to tell Josie.

"Tell Bo-Jeddy, 'Thanks very much'," said Josie politely, when Quinn told her. Then she thought for a bit and she added, "And tell him if he backs off it I'll get him every day for a trillion years, so he had better not."

She told her mother, and Mrs Swab sent round word to Bo-Jeddy's mum about how grateful she was to Christopher for helping out, and Bo-Jeddy was stuck with it because his mum wouldn't let him go sick on the day, which was the only get-out he could think of.

Bo-Jeddy's mum dressed him up herself and told him he looked a really lovely darling, which didn't please Bo-Jeddy one bit.

That's how Bo-Jeddy ended up in pink pants and gold shoes with buckles on and a scarlet cloak being Prince Charming while Josie was being the Sleeping Beauty on a camp-bed draped in roses for the procession. Mrs Swab had a flower shop, and she wanted to display her roses, that is why.

They won the Best Local Enterprise Float and got the first prize, which was twenty-five pounds.

So Bo-Jeddy got his picture in the *Grotley Gazette* in pink pants, except that the picture was in black-and-white, but everybody knew his pants were pink. The worst thing about it was that he got the picture taken *kissing* Josie.

The paper printed:

> Prince Charming (Christopher Bowater-Jennings) awakens The Sleeping Beauty (Josephine Mary Swab) with a kiss on the Prize-winning Town and Country Flowers Float at Grotley Town Parade.

Bo-Jeddy said kissing Josie was yeeeeeugh, but *that isn't the worst bit.*

The worst bit started after Bo-Jeddy got down from the float in John Bonzo Memorial Park.

He had his Man United bag with him, full of his clothes. He'd brought it along under the camp-bed on the float, so he wouldn't have to walk home in pink pants and a scarlet cloak.

Bo-Jeddy got up in the cab of the lorry to change.

He opened the bag.

His clothes weren't in the bag. Quinn had switched them for a frilly blue nightie that looked as if it belonged to somebody's mum. It had yellow roses round the neck and it came from Marks and Sparks.

Bo-Jeddy put his head out of the cab window, cautiously.

"Quinny?" he called. "Macmillan?"

They had both cleared off. So had Josie Swab and her mum.

Then the lorry man came back.

"Get dressed, son," he said. "I have to get back to the depot."

"I got no clothes," Bo-Jeddy told him.

"Then you'll have to go home the way you

are, won't you?" the lorry man said unkindly, and he turfed Bo-Jeddy out of his lorry.

That's how Bo-Jeddy ended up walking home round the side streets dressed as Prince Charming.

He managed to keep out of the way of most people he knew, till he got to his own street, Worby Drive.

Josie was there with her dog, and Macmillan and Quinn and Big Boots and Meatface. Big Boots and Meatface weren't meant to be there, but they'd heard the noise and come running.

Everyone cheered Bo-Jeddy.

Big Boots started singing, "One day my prince will come!" and all the neighbours came out of their doors to see what the fuss was.

Bo-Jeddy went scarlet.

"I'll flatten your face for you, Big Boots," he told Big Boots.

Considering Bo-Jeddy just about came up to Big Boots' knee-caps that didn't scare Big

Boots one bit.

Big Boots went on singing until Macmillan went over to sort him out, and by that time Bo-Jeddy was off down the road to his house.

Josie's dog yapped alongside him. It must have been the gold shoes that did it, or the pink pants. Bo-Jeddy could have had a go at kicking it, but he was afraid he would get bitten, because Josie's dog was like that.

His clothes were on the front step under a stone, where someone had put them. Bo-Jeddy picked them up and went inside. That was the end of it.

Bo-Jeddy never did figure out who switched his clothes for the blue nightie. He tucked the blue nightie in next door's bin by moonlight.

Two weeks later, Mrs Teresa Quinn gave up looking for her second-best Marks and Sparks blue nightie and bought herself another one, without telling her husband

Seamus. She never could work out how
the first one had gone walkies from the
washing-basket, but the new one was much
nicer.

That's how Quinn got his revenge on Bo-
Jeddy over the Crash Drivers business. Quinn
was clever like that, but a bit mean
sometimes too. Nobody is perfect, not even
Quinn.

That's the bad news.

The good news is that Bo-Jeddy got
something out of it all because Mrs Swab
sent Josie round with five pounds for Bo-
Jeddy, which was his cut of the first prize
winnings. Josie got five pounds from her
mum as well, but Mrs Swab kept the other
fifteen pounds herself.

Bo-Jeddy said that wasn't fair, considering
Josie's mum wasn't even on the float.

"OK, give me my mum's money back if
you don't want it!" Josie told him, but Bo-
Jeddy didn't.

He figured five pounds for wearing pink

pants and kissing Josie wasn't exactly
the rate for the job, but it was better than
nothing.

Big Boots
Isn't Sexy

Big Boots
Isn't Sexy

....

It's funny the way things go. One day nobody
had girlfriends and then Big Boots fell in love
with Marlene and after that everyone had to
have one. The trouble was that not everyone
could get one.

"Marlene's my woman," Big Boots went
around telling people.

"Stupid!" Macmillan said.

Then it turned out Marlene had a friend,
Cheryl, and Meatface said Cheryl was *his*
girlfriend, so the two biggest Bonzos both
had girlfriends.

"Bonzos have gone soft," Macmillan said,
and the next time he met Big Boots and
Meatface he did kissy-kissy at them.

Big Boots and Meatface went maniac and if
it hadn't been for Quinn's secret escape route
through the back yard at Nu Prices, next to

the Monaco Amusements, there might have been serious damage.

Then Big Boots got another one called Charlene from the Royals End, and Big Boots gave Marlene the shove. Marlene went round the place yelling that Big Boots was a creep. Then Charlene chucked Big Boots for not telling her about Marlene.

BIG BOOTS ISN'T SEXY got written up on the side wall of the Monaco, next to the swings, and everybody said it was Charlene or Marlene or maybe Quinn wrote it – but Quinn didn't, because it was written too high up for Quinn to reach. Then somebody changed ISN'T to IS, which was probably Big Boots himself, because nobody else thought he was sexy, not even Charlene and Marlene.

Next AVRIL LUVS MACMILLAN went up on the wall.

"Who is Avril?" Quinn asked Bo-Jeddy, but Bo-Jeddy didn't seem to know, and Quinn never asked Macmillan, just in case.

Macmillan saw it, and he got some stuff

and scrubbed it out.

Soon after that, Josie met Meatface down the pitch and putt and Meatface told Josie he fancied her.

"You're going out with Cheryl," Josie told him.

"Not any more," Meatface said. "I chucked her in."

"Well, you're not going out with me, no way!" Josie told him.

"Why not?" said Meatface.

And Josie told him. Then she told everybody else. That should have been the end of Meatface as a serious contender. Only Charlene didn't know. So Meatface and Charlene became a number.

Then Marlene and Big Boots got pally again. Both the Big Bonzo romances were on. Big Boots was kissy-kissy with Marlene and Meatface was wooing Charlene.

Big Boots and Meatface made sure everybody knew. They took their girlfriends out on their bikes together, and everybody saw them. Then Charlene fell off and had to have stitches, so even the grown-ups heard about it.

This may sound like a lot happening and it *was*, but it only took about four days to happen because they were all fast movers.

"What about us?" Bo-Jeddy said, when he met Quinn at the Monaco.

"What's what about us?" said Quinn.

"Well, the Bonzos got girlfriends," said Bo-Jeddy.

"Who needs them?" asked Quinn. "And what would you *do* with one if you had one?"

"Everything!" said Bo-Jeddy. "Like Big Boots."

"That's not what Marlene says Big Boots did," Quinn pointed out.

They both agreed Big Boots and Meatface were creeps.

"So are Marlene and Charlene creeps for going out with them," said Bo-Jeddy.

There was a long silence.

"You reckon Charlene would go out with me?" Bo-Jeddy asked Quinn.

Quinn was disgusted.

Next thing was Bo-Jeddy asked Charlene to chuck Meatface and go out with him instead and Charlene told him she only went out with men and then she told Meatface about Bo-Jeddy asking her.

The Bonzos came roaring down the Dump to sort it out, and Marlene and Charlene came with them.

"You lot leave our women alone!" Big Boots told Macmillan.

"Yeah!" yelled Marlene, from a safe distance.

"We got no time for baby boys!" Charlene shouted.

There would have been a fight, but old Eggy came out with his stick and broke it up.

"You got us in that," Macmillan accused Bo-Jeddy. "What you want to go chatting up Meatface's girl for?"

"'Cause you ain't got one and I ain't got one and little Quinny ain't got no chance of getting one, not ever!" Bo-Jeddy said miserably. "That's why! Everybody's got girlfriends but us."

The trouble was, it was true, and they all knew it.

"What about Avril?" Quinn said.

"Somebody made Avril up," Macmillan said glumly.

"Yeah," said Bo-Jeddy. Then he took a deep breath, and added defiantly: "Yeah. Somebody made her up. I did!"

"You creep!" said Macmillan, beginning to boil. If Bo-Jeddy didn't know he'd made a mistake admitting what he'd done, one look at Macmillan instantly convinced him.

"I only did it because Big Boots and Meatface have girlfriends and we haven't, and that makes it look like we're soft." Bo-Jeddy added quickly: "I made one up so one of us would have one, and you are the best-looking so I thought it would be you."

There was a long silence while Macmillan thought out what to say next and Quinn wondered how Macmillan could kid himself that he was good-looking.

"I ought to kill you," Macmillan said.

"Hold on," said Quinn, who didn't want to be mixed up in another boring old fight about nothing. "Maybe Bo-Jeddy is right, Macmillan."

"How right?" demanded Macmillan, who was really mad because it was his name went up on the Monaco and there wasn't any Avril but he'd been thinking there might be only he didn't know her right name and now he'd found out that there definitely wasn't, so he hadn't got a girlfriend even if he didn't know who she was.

"If everybody has one but us, we *ought* to have one," Quinn said.

"What ... between us?" gasped Macmillan.

"Girls don't work like that," said Bo-Jeddy. "I don't think so, anyway."

"One of us ought to have one," said Quinn.

"If one of us had one then we would be all right."

"Yeah," said Bo-Jeddy. "*Ought* to have one is great, but where do we get one? All the ones we know are booked already."

"What about Josie?" said Macmillan.

"You know what Josie said about Meatface," Bo-Jeddy pointed out.

"Yeah," said Macmillan. "Forget Josie. She's too tough."

"Josie might fix it for us, just the same," said Quinn.

"Yeah," said Bo-Jeddy. "Only I'm not asking Josie."

"Me neither!" said Macmillan, so it was down to Quinn as usual to handle the negotiations.

And Quinn did. Quinn asked Josie to fix them up.

"Yeah, easy," Josie said, unexpectedly. "How many do you want?"

"One each," said Quinn. He'd been planning to ask for one for Macmillan, but when Josie said *easy*, Quinn thought that he and Bo-Jeddy might as well have one too so they wouldn't be left out of it.

"What sort?" said Josie, as if she was selling things in a shop.

"Just girls," said Quinn, who hadn't got round to thinking what sort.

"What about ones with bikes?" suggested Josie, very casually, as if it didn't matter. Quinn should have twigged she was planning some joke, but he didn't.

"Why bikes?" said Quinn.

"Then you can do what Meatface and Big Boots did," Josie explained, slowly, as if he was dumb like Macmillan. "You ride round with them on your bikes. Then people know you've got girlfriends. That's what you want, isn't it?"

"What is?" said Quinn.

"You want girlfriends you're seen with so people know you've got one," Josie said with a grin. "Not ones you have to hug and kiss. Then you don't have to bother no more after you've showed them off, right?"

"Y-e-a-h! Yeah! Right!" said Quinn, because Josie had hit the nail on the head.

He went away thinking Josie was smarter than he'd thought she was, but he didn't reckon how smart, and he didn't catch on that it was a Josie-trap till later.

Josie brought the three girls down to the park with their bikes.

Two of them had bikes, though both the bikes had balancers on the back wheel.

The third one, the really *little* one, had a trike, and she had a yellow teddy taped to the handlebars.

"We're not going out with them!" Bo-Jeddy told Josie angrily. "They're *little*."

"You said girlfriends with bikes," Josie pointed out. "They're girls. And they're very friendly, and they've got bikes. Well, two bikes anyway. And it is a *big* tricycle."

"They're all babies!" Macmillan said in disgust.

"I'm six," the one with the tricycle said.

Josie started to giggle and then she took the little girls off for the ice-creams she had promised them, because she knew all along they wouldn't be going for bike rides with the Dump Gang, and so did the girls. That left Josie one up on the Dump Gang, and it made Macmillan's lot look really silly, so Josie thought it was worth three ice-creams.

"Josie's done us!" Bo-Jeddy said. "We're really really stuck because we've told everyone we'll be going out on bikes with our girlfriends and now we haven't got any and everyone will know."

"We got to destroy Josie!" Macmillan said.

Nobody thought much of that. Nobody had ever been much good at destroying Josie.

Then Marlene and Charlene came down to the shelter.

"Clear off!" Bo-Jeddy told them. "Go back to the Bonzos!"

"No way," said Marlene. "Josie sent us with a message."

"What message?" asked Macmillan.

"Josie said we was to tell you her Girls' Gang was finished with boyfriends. We *tried* boyfriends for our Baby Boyfriends Week and none of us liked them so now we're not having boyfriends no more. And Josie says you're not to worry about looking silly because the Bonzos will look sillier when you tell them Charlene and me said they was no use."

Then Marlene blew Macmillan a kiss and Charlene showed Bo-Jeddy the back of her knickers and they ran off to join Josie.

"I didn't know Josie *had* a Girls' Gang," Bo-Jeddy muttered, red in the face.

"Girls are stupid," Macmillan said bitterly.

"Let's go and tell Big Boots and Meatface that their girlfriends were having them on!" said Quinn.

Quinn was pleased because Big Boots and Meatface would look stupid, but he was a bit confused about Josie.

Quinn was beginning to think Josie might

be smarter than he was, as well as being tough. He also thought that *maybe* Josie fancied him as well, and was too shy to say so.

Anyone in Grotley could have told him that was rubbish. Josie could have buttered little Quinn and put him on toast and had him for her breakfast with three burgers for afters, but there was no harm in him thinking it anyway, and Quinn was always a bit of a dreamer.

The Three Camel Kid

The
Three Camel Kid

Everybody felt a bit silly after the Girls' Gang business, so Quinn came up with the Great Crash Driver's Dodge to get one over on the Bonzos.

"Leave Macmillan out of this one," Quinn told Bo-Jeddy. "He'd only muck it up. You and me will work this one all by our little selves."

"Who'll we do it on, Quinny?" Bo-Jeddy asked.

"Meatface," Quinn said. "Meatface is best, because he thinks he's the bee's knees at everything, so he won't spot it."

So they went down to the Monaco and hung about, hoping Meatface would walk in.

And Meatface did.

Quinn and Bo-Jeddy pretended they were so busy doing Crash Drivers that they didn't notice Meatface. That was all part of the plot, because they wanted him to bust in on them and start it.

"Go for it, Quinny!" Bo-Jeddy shouted.

Quinn was concentrating hard. The Rider Record on the top corner of the game screen showed he was second phase, 156 mph, and he had a Red Warning for running over a camel. Nobody hit camels in Crash Drivers. They were on screen so little kids could get the notion of how to steer round things before they went on the danger sections, like Desert Rumble and Peril Peaks and the Gaps of Death. Quinn had never, ever made it to the Gaps of Death, because of his legs being too short to work the pedals properly.

"Brilliant!" Bo-Jeddy said loudly, hoping Meatface was listening in, and by this time Meatface *was*.

"Doing well, ain't I?" Quinn muttered, through clenched teeth.

He hit another Camel.

"Tough luck," Bo-Jeddy said, patting his

back. Then Bo-Jeddy shouted, "Go on, Quinny my son! Go on, do it, DO IT!" for Meatface's benefit.

Quinn had roared up to 169mph which was just short of his limit, Quinn's limit being set where other people's limits began, because of his short legs.

BANG!

A third camel lay dead in the road, and Quinn's car plunged into the Crocodile Swamp with the machine flashing "YOU'RE DEAD MAN!" at him and the hooter going and the crocodiles eating the little yellow blob man that was supposed to be Quinn-rolled-out-of-his-roadster.

Quinn relaxed, with a smile of triumph on his face. He didn't have to act it, because for Quinn it was an above-average run, even allowing for the three dead camels.

"Great stuff, Quinny! Three camels!" Bo-Jeddy said. "Definitely a best ever on Crash Drivers!"

That brought Meatface over. Quinn knew

that it would.

"169 mph second phase and three camels, Quinny?" Meatface sneered. "Anybody can do that."

Quinn spun round on the driving seat to confront Meatface, narrowing his eyes and trying to look as if he was mad.

"Oh yeah?" Quinn said. "You want to make that a challenge?"

"Hold on, Meatface!" Bo-Jeddy said, coming in on cue. "You reckon you can take on the Dump Gang champ and beat him, right?"

"Yeah," Meatface said, confidently. "Yeah. I do."

"So it is an *official challenge*?" Bo-Jeddy said. "On behalf of the Bonzos?"

"Yeah!" Meatface said, his face lighting up. "Yeah! Yeah! Bonzos versus Dump Gang! That's it."

Next minute he had heaved Quinn out of the driving chair and he was off. Meatface got to Peril Peaks and then he slammed, banged off and was killed in Death Valley at 305 mph and no camels.

"Beat that!" he said, confidently, climbing out of the seat.

Bo-Jeddy slipped into position, flexing his fingers.

"*Official* challenge?" he told Meatface.

"Not *you* ... him!" Meatface blustered.

"You said you would beat the Dump Gang champ!" Bo-Jeddy spouted gleefully. "That's me, isn't it? Not the Three Camel Kid!" And he zoomed off through the camels as if they weren't there. Bo-Jeddy finished up 450 mph and the second Gap of Death with the vampire bats, no problem.

Meatface went beetroot, and stormed out of the Monaco.

So that was it. A win for Quinn's brain again.

Or it would have been, only Meatface got to Macmillan first, and Macmillan didn't know what had been going on, so he fell flat in it.

* * *

"Official challenge, Bonzos versus Dump Gang!" Macmillan came bouncing down to the Dump to tell Bo-Jeddy and Quinn. "Our team against their team at Crash Drivers! Brilliant, yeah?"

"Team?" Quinn said, aghast.

"Yeah," Macmillan said. "Best three players in each gang. And Josie Swab is being ref, so there won't be any cheating. Me and Meatface made up the rules. Our number one plays their number one..."

"That's me," Bo-Jeddy said, making a face. Big Boots was Crash Drivers King of the Monaco. Bo-Jeddy knew Big Boots could lick him any day, easy-peasy.

"Yeah, well ... guess who gets Meatface!" Macmillan said triumphantly. "*Me*, our number two, that's who! I can lick Meatface hollow, no bother!"

"That leaves Ratso and Marco and Dummy," Bo-Jeddy pointed out.

"Yeah, well. I can beat any of them,"

Macmillan said.

"Sure. *You* can, Macmillan. We know that. They're no use," Bo-Jeddy said. "You can and I can. But *we* won't be playing them, will we? I'm playing Big Boots and you've got Meatface. That leaves Quinny to play the last game."

"Trouble is, you can't count to three, Macmillan," Quinn said sourly.

"Eh?" said Macmillan.

"Big Boots beats Bo-Jeddy, right? One to them," Quinn said. "You maybe, *maybe* beat Meatface. So that is one all. Then the decider is *me*, right? Me against Ratso or Dummy or Marco. *Me,* the Three Camel Kid, with legs that can't reach the pedals ... so I *can't* win, can I?"

"The Bonzos win by two games to one!" Bo-Jeddy said.

"Yeah, yeah. But I'll beat Meatface, won't I, Quinny?" Macmillan objected.

"*Team* game, Macmillan," Quinn said. "You win, we lose. The Bonzos will go round boasting that they beat the Dump Gang hollow!"

"And we're stuck with it, because of you, Macmillan," Bo-Jeddy said bitterly.

"Yeah," Macmillan admitted, looking down in the mouth. "Yeah. Got it wrong, didn't I?"

"Lumbered us," Bo-Jeddy said. "You fink, Macmillan!"

"Who are you calling a fink?" Macmillan barked, blazing up.

"Hold on," Quinn said. "I got it! I got it figured!"

And he explained, quickly.

Everybody turned up for the challenge at the Monaco, as arranged. Big Boots had made sure of that, because he wanted everybody to see the Dump Gang getting stuffed.

"Read out the challenge rules, Josie, so there won't be any arguments afterwards," Quinn told her.

"'Only gang members officially registered as gang members may compete,'" Josie read out. "'Captains will hand over the team lists clearly written out to the ref.' That's me. 'Players will compete against each other in the order selected. All games to be played one after the other and no one interferes with play. No subs allowed on. Absolutely no changes whatsoever allowed to these rules so no one can say anyone cheated afterwards. By order of Big Boots and Macmillan. Signed Big Boots and Macmillan.'"

"Agreed?" Josie said.

"Yeah!" said Big Boots.

"Yeah!" said Macmillan.

"OK," Josie said. "Give me your team lists."

Big Boots was looking confident as he handed over the Bonzos' list. He knew he was on a winner.

1. Big Boots 2. Meatface 3. Ratso

Then Macmillan gave Josie the list Quinn had scribbled out.

1. Quinn 2. Bo-Jeddy 3. Macmillan

"Right," Josie said. "Here's the games,

-54-

according to your official team lists. Game One: Quinny plays Big Boots. Game Two: Bo-Jeddy plays Meatface. Game Three: Macmillan plays Ratso."

Big Boots wakened up, too late.

"It's a fix!" he yelled. "I'm changing our team order!"

"No way," Josie said. "I'm the ref. You agreed the rules. Absolutely no changes to the rules are permitted, you said. So the games are played off in team order and your team order is what I've got on your sheet so that is the way you are playing!"

"We been stung!" Big Boots grumbled.

Quinn was grinning all over his face.

"I'll beat you anyway, Quinny," Big Boots told him.

"Yeah," Quinny said. "But I don't mind losing, do I, if it means your team loses the match?"

And that's what happened, even though Macmillan nearly blew it by half-hitting a camel.

"2-1 to the Dump Gang!" Macmillan told Big Boots.

"And it's all down to the Three Camel Kid," Bo-Jeddy broke in.

"Who?" said Big Boots.

Big Boots and
the Grudge Match

Big Boots and the Grudge Match

....

The Dump Gang were down at the Dump counting their cans when Big Boots and Ratso turned up. They just walked on to the Dump, ducking under the fence, which wasn't the way the Bonzos usually did things. Quinn thought they'd gone mad.

"Listen," Big Boots told Macmillan, Bo-Jeddy and Quinn. "I met Stewarty. His school is challenging our school to a Big Grudge Match at American football like they have on TV. And it's tomorrow, ten o'clock on the Commons, old hockey pitch, so you've got to play or we get licked!"

"Yeah! Yeah! Right!" Macmillan said. Macmillan liked American football on TV because people charged about knocking each other over, and Macmillan was best at that.

"I'm captain because I'm oldest," Big

Boots told them. "That means I pick me as quarter back because I can throw the ball further than anybody else and Macmillan is the whatsit player that dashes up the field and catches the ball and knocks people over and scores touchdowns."

"Yeah! G-R-E-A-T!" breathed Macmillan, enthusiastically.

"If butterfingers can catch the ball," Quinn mumbled under his breath, but luckily Macmillan didn't hear him.

Quinn didn't fancy it. He'd seen American football on TV. People who were small and slow got sat on by people who were big and fast, and that was why Quinn didn't fancy it.

Quinn was too bright to get himself sat on by the mob from Stewarty's school, so he set out to fix it.

He got hold of Josie.

"You're big and tough and can duff anybody, Josie," he told her, after he'd explained about the match. "Right?"

"Right, Quinny," Josie said.

"And you don't want to see our school duffed by Stewarty's school, do you?"

"No," said Josie.

"So we need you in our team instead of me," Quinn said.

Josie thought about it. "Big Boots has it in for me, after the Crash Drivers," she said. "And Big Boots is captain, so he picks the team, right? So I don't think I'll get playing."

"You say you'll play, and I'll sort it out," Quinn told her.

"OK, I'll play," Josie said.

So the next morning when the two school teams showed up on the Commons, Josie Swab was there with her brother Billy's old football boots that she'd found in the potting shed.

"Josie is bigger than me. So if she plays we've more chance of winning," Quinn told Big Boots, interrupting his captain's orders. Big Boots was bossing everybody around as usual, but nobody could do anything about it, because Big Boots had told Macmillan that Macmillan was the big cheese who would score all the touchdowns, and for once Macmillan was on his side.

"She's a girl. There's no way I'm having a girl in my team," Big Boots said. "You're just yellow, Quinny. You want out."

Quinny wasn't surprised. He'd known all along that Big Boots wouldn't let Josie on the team if he could help it.

"Well, I told Josie she could play," he said. "What am I going to tell her then, if you say she can't?"

"Tell her to bug off!" Big Boots said.

"*You* tell her!" Quinn said. "I don't want her sitting on my head!"

"Yeah, you tell her, Big Boots," Meatface said, because like everybody else he was fed up with Big Boots giving Captain's orders all day. He thought maybe Big Boots would tell her and then Josie would duff him and it would be a good fight, and Big Boots would lose and that would stop him being so bossy next time.

"You tell her, Macmillan," Big Boots said.

But Macmillan wasn't silly enough to do that without life insurance, which he hadn't got.

"Ratso?" Big Boots said, but Ratso had gone off to the bog.

"You tell her, Dummy," Big Boots said, but even Dummy wasn't that stupid.

"She's brought her brother's boots and everything and she's *expecting* to play," Quinn said.

Big Boots protested, but nobody was going to do his dirty work for him, so he had another think. He had to tell Josie she wasn't playing, but make it sound as if she maybe *might* be so she wouldn't duff him.

"You can be sub," he told Josie, getting ready to duck. "You get on if I decide on a tactical switch or somebody gets hurt." What Big Boots meant was you-get-on-only-if-somebody-gets-hurt-like-*dead*, but he didn't say so to Josie.

"Otherwise I don't get on?" Josie said,

flexing her muscles.

"Well ... er..." Big Boots started to retreat.

"Right, Captain!" Josie said. "Whatever you say, Captain." Big Boots galloped away onto the field, wondering what Josie was sickening for and whether it was catching.

"OK, Josie?" Quinn said.

"I'm sub," Josie grinned. "Just like you thought I would be."

So the two teams lined up, and Josie wasn't on, and Quinn was, which he didn't want to be, and wasn't going to be for any longer than he could help.

"No one tell Stewarty we've a girl as sub, or he'll call us Knickers United!" Captain Big Boots told his team.

So they lined up and Big Boots big booted the ball up the other team's end. Stewarty caught it and put his head down and crashed off on a bull-run.

C-R-U-N-C-H! B-A-N-G! S-M-A-C-K!

Everybody flattened everybody. It was an excuse for a fight really, which was what

Quinn thought it would be, but the surprise was that Quinn charged straight into it.

That was a big pile of players fighting for the ball, and Quinn was in there, underneath.

When they all climbed off, Quinn was lying flat on his back with his nose bleeding buckets.

Macmillan picked Quinn up.

"You all right, Quinn?" he asked. "Who punched you? I'll get him for you!"

There was blood all down Quinn's Man United jersey.

Quinn said, "Where am I?"

"Eh?" said Big Boots.

"Did I fall and hurt myself?" Quinn asked shakily.

Then he sat down and put his hand carefully to his face, and when he took his hand away there was buckets more blood than before, great big slithers of it.

"I don't feel well," Quinn gulped. "I think I'm going to be sick!"

And he made chokey noises, throwing his

head in Big Boots' direction.

Bo-Jeddy and Macmillan carried him off and gave him to Marlene to look after.

That's how Josie ended up playing after all.

Which is why Stewarty's school got licked, because Josie was too tough for everybody and she got four touchdowns and a conversion.

So that was all right.

Quinn went home with Marlene and Josie after the game and his nose didn't bleed any more. He kept telling people what a pity it was that he'd had to come off, but maybe it was a good thing because it meant the team won.

Quinn was well pleased with himself.

He had only one problem left: strawberry jam is dead sticky, and there was strawberry jam all down the front of his Man United strip. The way Quinny had planned things he was going to be OK because Man United play in red but it didn't work because Man United red doesn't have pips in it, and strawberry jam does.

Nosebleed blood doesn't have pips in it either, but Quinn had reckoned that Big Boots and his mates wouldn't spot it when they were getting him off the pitch and Marlene wasn't going to tell because she was in the plot with Josie and Quinn.

"You should have used tomato soup," Josie told him. "It's more like blood."

"Mum only had chicken broth in the cupboard," Quinn told her. "So I had to use jam."

So it didn't make sense when Marlene and Charlene and Josie went round making chicken broth noises at Quinn for weeks afterwards.

Nobody knew what they meant except Quinn, and he wasn't going to say, in case Big Boots found out he'd been fooled.

The Mushroom
Trillionaires

The Mushroom Trillionaires

Quinn thought he was smart, but he didn't always get it right. One time he got it very wrong was with the mushrooms.

Old Eggy got some mushroom compost from the mushroom man to put on his plants, but the mushroom compost didn't help the plants much. Old Eggy's whole allotment came up mushrooms, big white ones, about twenty centimetres across.

Eggy was stamping round his allotment calling the mushrooms names when Quinn heard him.

"Bleeding mushrooms!" Old Eggy was shouting, hitting them with his stick. Little bits of white mushroom were flying everywhere.

"What's wrong with them, Eggy?" Quinn asked him over the fence.

"What's bleeding well right with them!" growled Eggy. "Compost's full of their spores. Isn't supposed to be, but it is. Now I got tons of mushrooms I don't want. And they take a lot of picking. How can I go picking mushrooms with my bleeding back?"

"OK, Eggy," said Quinn. "We'll pick them for you."

He went and hauled Bo-Jeddy and Macmillan out of the Monaco Amusements.

"Old Eggy's allotment is full of mushrooms," he told Bo-Jeddy.

"So?" said Macmillan.

"So we pick them for Eggy, and then we'll have trillions of mushrooms," Quinn announced.

"Great," said Bo-Jeddy.

"Don't like mushrooms," Macmillan said.

"You don't have to like them, Macmillan," Quinn told him.

"If I don't like them I'm not going to eat them," Macmillan said.

"Nobody's going to eat them," Quinn said,

impatiently. "We pick them, we pack them, and we sell them to the shops."

"R-i-g-h-t!" said Bo-Jeddy, getting the idea at once.

"Then somebody's going to eat them," Macmillan said slowly. "You said *nobody* was going to eat them, but *somebody* is."

The other two weren't listening. They were busy planning Dump Gang Mushroom Marketing, Inc., so they could make a lot of money to spend in Monaco Amusements.

"Equal shares," said Quinn. "Because we're all in this together."

"Right," said Bo-Jeddy. "We'll be mushroom trillionaires!"

"All we need is a bucket," they told Macmillan. "We get a bucket and we pile the mushrooms in and we take them round the shops and we sell them, right?"

"You can borrow one of my mum's buckets," said Macmillan, which is what they hoped he would say, because his house was nearest to the Dump and they couldn't be bothered walking to their houses. "There's plenty of buckets round our place."

Macmillan ran home and got a bucket from his house and they filled it right to the top with mushrooms and there were still tons of mushrooms left, so they got another bucket from Macmillan's house and filled it and then they got fed up because the buckets were too small.

"Old Eggy's compost came in sacks," Quinn pointed out, so they went to Old Eggy's shed and knocked him up from his afternoon sleep and he let them have a plastic compost sack to cart the rest of the mushrooms away, but they didn't tell him about selling the mushrooms to the shops.

"Selling them doesn't seem fair on Old Eggy," Bo-Jeddy said. "He ought to get some of the money."

"Yeah," said Macmillan. "They're his mushrooms 'cause they grew in his allotment."

"Eggy's cut is getting his mushrooms

picked for free," Quinn told the others firmly. They thought about it, and then they agreed that that was fair, because the compost was heavy and smelly and they had had to wade around in it up to their ankles, pulling mushrooms in the hot sun.

"Now we take them to shops and sell them," Quinn said.

"Who does?" said Bo-Jeddy.

"We does," said Quinn. "All of us."

So they did.

None of the supermarkets would buy any mushrooms because they all got theirs from central suppliers and the man at Archie Logan's Green Meadow Fruits was rude and said he didn't want to poison his customers and Mrs Swami chased them off because she thought they were in to nick grapes. In the end there was only Skid left.

They went to Skid's stall in the market, and they showed him some of the mushrooms in Bo-Jeddy's bucket.

Skid up-ended the bucket on a bit of paper

beside his stall, to take a proper look at them, because he didn't want his customers poisoned either.

"The ones at the bottom are all black," Skid told them.

"Eh?" said Quinn.

"Looks like soot to me," said Skid. "Don't reckon I can sell sooty mushrooms."

"It's coal dust that, not soot!" said Macmillan indignantly, but Skid wasn't having any.

"What did you get us a coal bucket for, Macmillan?" Bo-Jeddy demanded, when they'd cleared off.

"Because it was better than the lime bucket," Macmillan said. "I had to pick some bucket, didn't I? You said a bucket. So I got you the coal bucket because it was better than the lime bucket. Then you said another bucket, so I got you the lime bucket too. So there."

"Lime!" said Bo-Jeddy." Lime and coal. Nobody's going to buy lime and coal-covered mushrooms."

"Clean them and wash them properly," said Quinn. "Then bag them up."

"How?" said Bo-Jeddy. "What in?"

"Rubbish sacks," said Quinn. "The cheapy ones people use for rubbish."

Quinn and Bo-Jeddy went to scrounge some black rubbish sacks and they left Macmillan to take the mushrooms back to his house and clean them when his mother was out.

"We got the bags, you put them in!" they told Macmillan when they arrived back.

"That's not fair," said Macmillan.

"You mucked it up with the buckets," they told him. "So it is fair."

Macmillan thought about duffing them, but he didn't. He usually would have, but he felt a bit stupid about the buckets.

Macmillan stuck some of the mushrooms in two rubbish sacks, and Quinn and Macmillan took them back to Skid. Bo-Jeddy didn't come. He said he had to go home because *Mindbenders* was on TV and he'd forgotten to tell his mum to record it.

"Then Macmillan and I get the money," Quinn told him. "You're O-U-T of the deal."

Quinn and Macmillan went back to Skid.

"Look at that, Skid," Quinn said, holding one of the sacks open. "Mushrooms clean as a whistle."

"All washed in disinfectant!" Macmillan said proudly.

"Smells like it too," said Skid, and he wouldn't buy the mushrooms.

"Coal-dust and lime and disinfectant!" Quinn said, despairingly, when he got Macmillan away from the stall.

"You said wash them and clean them," said Macmillan. "So I washed them. And you need disinfectant to clean them properly. And I used the best stuff my mum keeps under the sink so I'd get it right, and now you don't like it!"

He went off in a huff.

Quinn tipped the two sacks of mushrooms

into a street bin, and then he went off to find Bo-Jeddy, who hadn't gone home after all – that was all lies. He was just fed up trying to sell mushrooms that nobody wanted.

Bo-Jeddy was at the Dump banging bits off his bike. They had hidden the compost bag with the last of the mushrooms down by the oil drums where the Bonzos wouldn't see it, and Quinn dragged Bo-Jeddy down that way to check it.

"We still got a big lot in that compost bag," Quinn explained hopefully. "And it is a really good idea selling them. Maybe we can pick some more tomorrow."

"Forget it, Quinn," said Bo-Jeddy.

Quinn opened the bag.

The inside of the bag had become very hot, because it was a plastic bag and they'd left it in the sun. There must have been creepy-crawlies on the mushrooms to begin with, because when Quinn opened it he saw that there were more creepy-crawlies in it than there were mushrooms.

"We could clean them," Quinn said hopefully. "Wash the creepy-crawlies off, and then sell the mushrooms. Just water we use. Not disinfectant."

"You wash them," said Bo-Jeddy, and he went off again.

Quinn was left with a great big bag full of creepy-crawlies and mushrooms, and no mates to help him, so he chucked the mushrooms on the Dump because he was fed up.

Next time he met Eggy, Old Eggy said, "There's more mushrooms come up in my compost," and he waited to see if Quinn would offer to come and pick them.

Quinn did.

Quinn did it because he was fond of Old Eggy, and he felt sorry about Eggy's back hurting and his allotment being spoiled. When Quinn had finished he threw the rotten things on the Dump, because he'd had enough of the mushroom business, then he went off for a swim in the river because it was a hot day for picking mushrooms.

Big Boots and Meatface came along later, to see if Macmillan's lot had put anything on the Dump that they could wreck.

They found a pile of old mushrooms, with loads of creepy-crawlies marching over it.

Big Boots didn't mind creepy-crawlies. He was used to them because his dad liked fishing, and he paid Big Boots for finding surface bait.

So Big Boots got a shovel and stuck the creepy-crawlies in a bait bag and got two pounds for them from his dad. Big Boots gave Meatface fifty pence as his cut, because Meatface only did the shovelling. It was Big Boots who pulled off the deal.

Clever clogs like Quinn don't always win, and maybe Big Boots and Meatface weren't as dumb as Quinn thought they were.

The Top Secret
Super Mega Hut

The Top Secret Super Mega Hut

One day Macmillan, Bo-Jeddy and Quinn were down at the Dump looking at where their hut ought to be, but it wasn't, because of the Bonzos smashing it.

"Big Boots and Meatface doing our hut don't mean we can't have no hut never," Quinn said.

He was *really* missing the hut.

"It's OK having a hut," said Bo-Jeddy. "But how do we stop them smashing it?"

"Have a hut they can't get into," said Macmillan. "Up a tree or something."

"If we can get into it, so can they too," Bo-Jeddy pointed out. "How about a hut with a key?"

"I thought of that," Quinn said. "Trouble is a key means a door. And a door means walls. And if there are doors and walls, then Big

Boots and Meatface will knock them down, the same way they knocked down the other one."

"Well, suppose our hut was somewhere else?" Bo-Jeddy said, thinking maybe they could put it in somebody's garden, if they knew anybody who had a garden to spare and didn't mind people building a hut in it.

"It's got to be on the Dump," Quinn said passionately. "We're the Dump Gang so it has got to be on the Dump. Nowhere else is as good as the Dump. The Dump's our place."

"Quinny's dead right," announced Macmillan, and that sealed it.

Macmillan could see that Quinn absolutely needed to have another hut. Deep down they all did, but Quinn needed it more than most.

"You work on it, Quinny," Macmillan told him.

"Yeah," said Bo-Jeddy. "You're the one that's fussed."

"I'm fussed too," Macmillan told him,

though he wasn't, not all that much.

Quinn went off up Everest, and sat in the armchair, looking down at the Dump.

There was Dump all round. Piles of stuff and rubbish and plastic sacks and bits of old beds and bricks and great big half-sections of plastic pipes from the road development and even a bit of an old digger, yellow in some bits and rusted away in others.

Quinn looked and he looked and then he GOT IT!

Quinn was off down Everest in a flash, and back to the others. They were counting cans again. They got twenty pence for a hundred aluminium ones, and fifteen pence for tin, so they were always busy about the cans.

"What do the Bonzos bust up?" he asked the others.

"Our huts!" said Bo-Jeddy and Macmillan.

Then Quinn told them what he'd figured.

"We build a hut but they don't know it's a hut," he explained. "They don't know it is there. So they don't smash it up!"

"Yeah! Great!" said Macmillan.

"Oh, brilliant," said Bo-Jeddy. "What do we do then? Build a hut with a sign that says 'THIS ISN'T A HUT' on it?"

"Our hut is going to be an invisible hut," said Quinn.

"Better still," said Bo-Jeddy, "the sign can say 'YOU CAN'T SEE THIS HUT BECAUSE IT'S INVISIBLE'."

Macmillan thought that was very funny, but Quinn didn't. Quinn was dead serious.

"Like in the war films," he explained. "Camouflage. A hut that doesn't look like a hut. A hut with no door and no walls."

"How do we build a hut with no door and no walls, Quinny?" asked Macmillan, sounding dead puzzled because he was.

"We don't *build* it," said Quinn. "If we build it, it is going to be here and they are going to *see* it. Big Boots will come and he will say: 'What's that? Looks like doors and walls which means a hut.' And he will look and he will see our stuff inside and he will smash it, right?"

"Right," said the others.

"So we don't build it. We just move in!" said Quinn.

And he showed them.

What Quinn showed them was the leftover half-sections of pipe from the road development. They were about three metres across and they stood up-ended down at the far side of the Dump, all grouped together.

Quinn put two halves together and sat there, completely hidden.

"A hut with no door!" he said. "You get in through the roof."

"It's got walls, though," Macmillan objected.

"Not walls Big Boots can *see*," Quinn said. "All he sees is the old pipes that have been standing here for ever, not new walls. He doesn't know it's the walls of our hut. Like you said, Bo-Jeddy, he can't see our hut because it isn't there."

"Only it is," objected Macmillan.

"Yeah, but if he can't see it, it *isn't* as far as Big Boots is concerned. Am I right?"

Macmillan and Bo-Jeddy thought about it.

"It's only a one-man hut," Bo-Jeddy pointed out. "We're supposed to be a gang. We can't have three little one-man huts when we are supposed to be together."

"You don't see nothing, do you?" said Quinn impatiently. "We just rearrange them. And there's eight of them, so we can have the biggest HQ hut ever and from the outside no one will know, because it will still look like the old pipes standing there on their ends."

Everybody thought it was great, this time.

They put all their stuff in the hut. The tin cans and the bits of bike and Bo-Jeddy's briefcase for his sandwiches but he hadn't got any sandwiches and the Blaster and the Zig-Zag and the black sacks left over from the mushroom operation.

"OK," said Macmillan. "Now we got a hut, what do we do?"

"Test drive it," said Quinn. "But first we

got to build a hut."

"Eh?" said Macmillan, who didn't think he'd heard right. "What for? We got a hut, without building it."

"We build another one that *looks* like a hut!" said Quinn.

Bo-Jeddy had already got the idea, because he knew the way Quinn's mind worked, sort of, but they had to spell it out for Macmillan.

First they did the building, and then it was time for the test drive.

Bo-Jeddy and Quinn went up to the Monaco.

They did Crash Drivers, as usual. Neither of them were as good as their best, but that was because they were too busy talking.

Things like: *"Reckon the new hut's great."*

And *"Best hut ever, Quinny!"*

Stuff like that.

Meatface was there, tucked in behind the Alpine Skier.

Quinn knew he was there, that was what the talking was for.

"Don't say nothing to Big Boots!" Bo-Jeddy warned Quinn, very loudly. It was so loud that Quinn thought Bo-Jeddy might have given the game away. Then he remembered how stupid Meatface was and thought it was probably all right.

Bo-Jeddy and Quinn bunged off.

Meatface went and got Big Boots.

"They done a new hut and it's camouflaged like the war films so it doesn't look like a hut but it *is* their hut and we should do it," Meatface told Big Boots.

"We do it when I decide to do it," said Big Boots, asserting his authority.

"Yeah, well—" Meatface began.

"Like *now*!" said Big Boots.

So at round about half past four Big Boots and Meatface and the rest of the Bonzo mob came creeping over the wire, under the trunk, down the pipe and round the back of the hedge. Meatface had found out that that was the path the Dump Gang used and so the Bonzos used it too, just to prove they were the kings, even in the Dump Gang's own land.

"We're looking for a hut that doesn't look like a hut," said Big Boots.

"If we don't know what it looks like, how can we spot it?" said Meatface.

"Easy," said Big Boots. "They only just built it, so it wasn't there before. All we do is spy out what's new. What's new has got to be it."

So they did.

And there was a new pile of old tyres and stuff up by the hedgerow with an old tarpaulin cover that made it look just like an ordinary pile *but* you knew it was a new hut trying to look like it wasn't a new hut *if* you knew that was the kind of new hut you were looking for, which Big Boots did.

"Charge!" Big Boots shouted, and they got planks and sticks and stuff and they started tearing the hut apart.

BIFF BANG WALLOP! Big Boots and his mob started bashing.

Then the wasps got going.

It was Bo-Jeddy who thought of building where the wasps' nest was in the hedge. Quinn had been figuring on a booby trap with water and stuff, but the wasps were better.

Dummy got three on his nose and there were more down Meatface's back and Marco got stung on his arms and legs. Ratso got away with a big scare and no stings but Big Boots really bought it.

Big Boots was furthest in, smashing round him with his plank, so Big Boots got most of the wasps coming out of the hedge. There was a lot of Big Boots to sting so a lot of them went for him and he was yelling and screeching and then the best ever happened.

Big Boots GOT STUNG ON THE BUM!

He ran off yelling with the mob after him.

"Yo-Yo-Yo!" yelled Bo-Jeddy, sticking his head up from the Top Secret Super Mega Hut that the Bonzos hadn't even suspected was there.

"Dump Gang are the champions!" chanted Macmillan.

"That done them!" said Quinn, with quiet satisfaction.

He was right to be satisfied. Big Boots and his mob were strong so they won most times when it came to battles, but that was just muscle, not brain. The Dump Gang was better, because they had Macmillan for the muscle and Bo-Jeddy for the bits between, and best of all they had Quinn, and his brain.

That's why the Dump Gang always wound up top of the pile.

CAPTURE BY ALIENS!

Eric Johns

When Zallie has to stay at home and look after her little brother Dessie instead of joining the crowds awaiting the arrival of the Alien Federation, she thinks she's missing out on an adventure. But, suddenly, the two children find themselves herded like cows on board an enormous flying saucer and in peril of their lives... Who are their hooting alien captors? And how can Zallie and Dessie escape? There's lots to think about and enjoy in this gripping science-fiction story.

THE AMAZING ADVENTURES
OF IDLE JACK

Robert Leeson

"Keep your eyes open, smile nicely and never disagree with anybody," Jack's mother tells him when she sends her idle son off to school. And it proves good advice, too, through the amazing adventures that follow, as Jack becomes star pupil, goes out to work, attends his own funeral and finds himself suitor to a princess!

Embellished with elements from a number of classic popular stories, this is a deliciously airy new version of a favourite folk-tale by the author of *Smart Girls*.

CREEPE HALL

Alan Durant

If you like vampires, ghosts, mummies, batty boffins, werebadgers and crazy fun-filled adventures, then Creepe Hall is the place for you!

MY AUNTY SAL AND THE
MEGA-SIZED MOOSE

Martin Waddell

Aunty Sal just loves adventure. She's got a real nose for trouble, too. Together with her pal Erwin, she searches for treasure and meets a mega-sized moose; she gets caught up with an eagle and a polar bear; she takes on a blood-thirsty band of pirates on the Spanish Main and has a showdown in the Last Chance Saloon with the fearsome Killer McGill... According to Uncle Jack, Aunty Sal's stories are all hogwash but, true or not, these tall tales are the funniest, most dang entertaining you could wish for.

MORE WALKER PAPERBACKS
For You to Enjoy

Books by the same author

Fred the Angel
Little Obie and the Flood
Little Obie and the Kidnap
The Owl and Billy Stories
The Adventures of Pete and Mary Kate
My Aunty Sal and the Mega-sized Moose

THE DUMP GANG

Class No. ___J___   Acc No. _C115462_

Author: _waddell, M_   Loc: _FEB 2002_

LEABHARLANN
CHONDAE AN CHABHAIN

1. **This book may be kept three weeks. It is to be returned on / before the last date stamped below.**
2. **A fine of 20p will be charged for every week or part of week a book is overdue.**

	/ / JAN 2003	